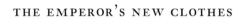

THE EMPEROR'S NEW CLOTHES

HANS CHRISTIAN
ANDERSEN

THE EMPEROR'S
NEW CLOTHES

Translated and illustrated
by Erik Blegvad

HARCOURT, BRACE & WORLD, INC.
New York

also translated and illustrated by Erik Blegvad

Hans Christian Andersen's THE SWINEHERD

© *1959 by Erik Blegvad*
All rights reserved. No part of this book may be reproduced in
any form or by any mechanical means, including mimeograph and
tape recorder, without permission in writing from the publisher.

Library of Congress Catalog Card Number: 59-8948
Printed in the United States of America

ANY years ago there lived an emperor who was so immensely fond of beautiful new clothes that he spent all his money on being splendidly dressed. He had no interest in his soldiers; he did not care for the theater or for drives in the park except, and only, for showing off his new clothes. He had a robe for every hour of the day, and just as it might be said of some king, "He is in his council," it was always said here, "The Emperor is in his wardrobe!"

Much festivity went on in the big city where he lived, and many strangers arrived there every day. One such day there came two swindlers; they claimed to be weavers and said that they knew how to weave the most wonderful cloth imaginable. Not only were the colors and patterns something uncommonly beautiful to see, but also clothes sewn from their cloth had the extraordinary quality of being invisible to anyone either badly suited for his position or unforgivably stupid.

7

"Well those, of course, would be marvelous clothes," thought the Emperor. "Wearing those, I could discover who in my empire is not fit for the post he holds; I could tell the wise from the stupid. Yes, that cloth must be woven for me at once!" And he paid the two swindlers a lot of money in order that they could begin their work.

They actually did set up two looms, then pretended to be working, though they had absolutely nothing in the frames. Right off they demanded the finest silk and the most magnificent gold thread; this they put into their own bags, though still working their empty looms even far into the night.

"Now I should certainly like to know how far along they are with that cloth!" thought the Emperor. But it made him a bit uneasy to think that anyone stupid or at all unsuited

for his position would be unable to see it—not that he himself need worry (he felt pretty confident about that!). All the same he had better send someone else first to see how matters stood. The whole city knew of the extraordinary powers invested in this cloth, and everyone was eager to

see how inefficient or stupid his neighbor was.

"I will send my trustworthy old Prime Minister to the weavers," said the Emperor to himself. "He, better than anyone, will be able to see how the cloth looks, for he has good sense and nobody fills his post better than he!"

So off he went, the trusted old Prime Minister, to the hall where the two swindlers sat and worked at their empty looms. "Good heavens!" thought the old man, opening his eyes very wide. "I can't see a thing!" but he didn't say that.

Both swindlers begged him to be good enough to step up close, then asked, was it not a beautiful pattern and were not the colors delightful? All the time they were pointing

at the empty loom and the poor old minister kept peering as hard as he could, but he could see nothing, for there was nothing. "Good gracious me!" he thought. "Could I possibly be stupid? I never thought I was. Nobody must ever know! Or is it possible that I am badly suited to my office? Oh, no, it will never do for me to admit that I do not see the material!"

"Well, you say nothing about it," said the one who was weaving.

"Oh, why it's charming! Absolutely adorable!" said the old minister, squinting through his spectacles. "This pattern! And these colors! Yes, I shall certainly report to the Emperor that it pleases me enormously!"

"Ah, we are happy to hear that!" said both weavers, and then they commented on the curious design and the colors, naming them. The old minister listened carefully so that he might be able to repeat it all when he got home to the Emperor—and that's just what he did.

Now the swindlers demanded more money, more silk and gold, which they needed for the weaving. They put everything into their own pockets; not a single thread went on the loom. But they continued as before, weaving on the empty loom.

Soon the Emperor sent yet another honest official to see how the weaving was getting along and whether the cloth might be ready soon. He fared no better than the Prime Minister. He looked and looked, but as there was nothing but the empty frames, he could see nothing.

"There now! Isn't that a piece of handsome stuff!" said both swindlers, pointing out and explaining the lovely design, which did not exist at all.

"Stupid I am not!" thought the man. "Am I then unfit for my excellent position? That's curious! Of course it won't do to let anyone suspect!" Whereupon he praised the cloth he did not see and assured them of his delight in the pretty shades and lovely patterns. "Yes, it's absolutely adorable!" he told the Emperor.

The whole city was talking about the marvelous cloth.

The Emperor now wanted to see it for himself while it was still on the loom. With a whole crowd of selected gentlemen, among which were the two poor old officials who had been there before, he visited the crafty swindlers

who were weaving away for all they were worth, but without shred or thread.

"Yes, is it not *magnifique?*" asked the two honest officials. "May it please Your Majesty, observe. . . . Such a design! Such colors!" And they pointed to the empty loom, believing that others could probably see the cloth.

"What's this!" thought the Emperor. "I see nothing! But that's awful! Am I stupid? Am I not fit to be Emperor? That would be the most appalling thing that could ever befall me!—Oh, it's very beautiful!" said the Emperor. "It

has our most gracious approval!" And he nodded content-
edly, looking at the empty loom; he was not going to admit
that he could not see anything. His whole retinue, all the

people he had brought along, looked and looked but had
no more success than anybody else. However, like the
Emperor, they said, "Oh, it's very beautiful!" And they
advised him to use this fabulous new material for a suit he

could wear for the first time in the grand procession that would soon take place. "It's *magnifique!* Delicious! *Superbe!*" were the comments running from mouth to mouth, and everyone was just enchanted with the whole thing. The Emperor awarded each of the swindlers a Knight's Cross to hang from his buttonhole, and bestowed on them the title of Knights-of-the-Loom.

The entire night before the morning of the procession the two swindlers sat up with more than sixteen candles burning. People could see that they were busy trying to get the Emperor's new clothes finished in time. They pretended to be taking the cloth from the loom; they snipped at the air with large scissors; they sewed away with needles without thread; and at last they said, "There! The clothes are ready!"

The Emperor, with his most distinguished gentlemen-in-waiting, arrived in person. The two Knights-of-the-Loom each lifted an arm, as if they were holding something between them, and said, "Look, here are the trousers! Here's the frock! Here's the robe!" and so forth and so on. "It's as light as a cobweb! It feels as if one had nothing on at all;

but that's just the beauty of it!"

"Quite!" answered all the gentlemen, but they could see nothing, for there was nothing.

"Would it please Your Gracious Majesty to remove your clothes now?" asked the swindlers. "Then we shall fit the new ones on Your Majesty over here by the large mirror!"

The Emperor took off all his clothes, and the rascals pretended to be handing him each piece of the new ones they were supposed to have sewn. They reached around his middle and made motions as if tying something on; that was the train, and the Emperor twisted and turned in front of the mirror.

"Good gracious me, how it suits Your Majesty! How nicely it fits!" they all said. "What a pattern! Such colors! These are elegant clothes!"

"The canopy to be carried above Your Majesty in the procession is waiting outside," said the Imperial-Chief-Master-of-Ceremonies.

"Yes, as you see, I'm all ready!" said the Emperor. "Doesn't it fit well?" And he made yet another turn in front of the mirror, for he wanted it to look as if he were really admiring his finery.

The chamberlains who were supposed to carry the train
ran their hands along the floor as if to lift the train; they
walked off holding the air, not daring to let anyone suspect
that they could not see anything.

And so the Emperor walked in the procession under the lovely canopy, while all the crowds in the street and all the people at their windows said, "Heavens! How marvelous the Emperor's new clothes look! Such a beautiful train on those robes! How exquisitely it fits!" No one wanted it thought that he could not see anything, as that would make him somebody who was either very stupid or badly fitted for his position. None of the Emperor's clothes had ever before been such a success.

"But he has nothing on!" said a little child.

"Good heavens, listen to the voice of innocence!" said the father, and the child's remark was whispered from one to another.

"He has nothing on! That's what a little child is saying: 'He has nothing on!'"

"He has nothing on!" shouted everybody in the end. And the Emperor cringed inside himself, for it seemed to him that they were right; but he thought like this: "I shall have to go through with the procession."

And then he held himself even more proudly erect, and the chamberlains walked on behind him carrying the train that was not there at all.